Read for a Better World™

ASTRONAUTS

A First Look

PERCY LEED

GRL Consultants,
Diane Craig and Monica Marx,
Certified Literacy Specialists

Lerner Publications ◆ Minneapolis

Educator Toolbox

Reading books is a great way for kids to express what they're interested in. Before reading this title, ask the reader these questions:

What do you think this book is about? Look at the cover for clues.

What do you already know about astronauts?

What do you want to learn about astronauts?

Let's Read Together

Encourage the reader to use the pictures to understand the text.

Point out when the reader successfully sounds out a word.

Praise the reader for recognizing sight words such as *who* and *they*.

TABLE OF CONTENTS

Astronauts

An astronaut is a person who travels into space.

How do you think a person gets ready to be an astronaut?

Astronauts travel to space in spaceships. The ships are powered by rockets.

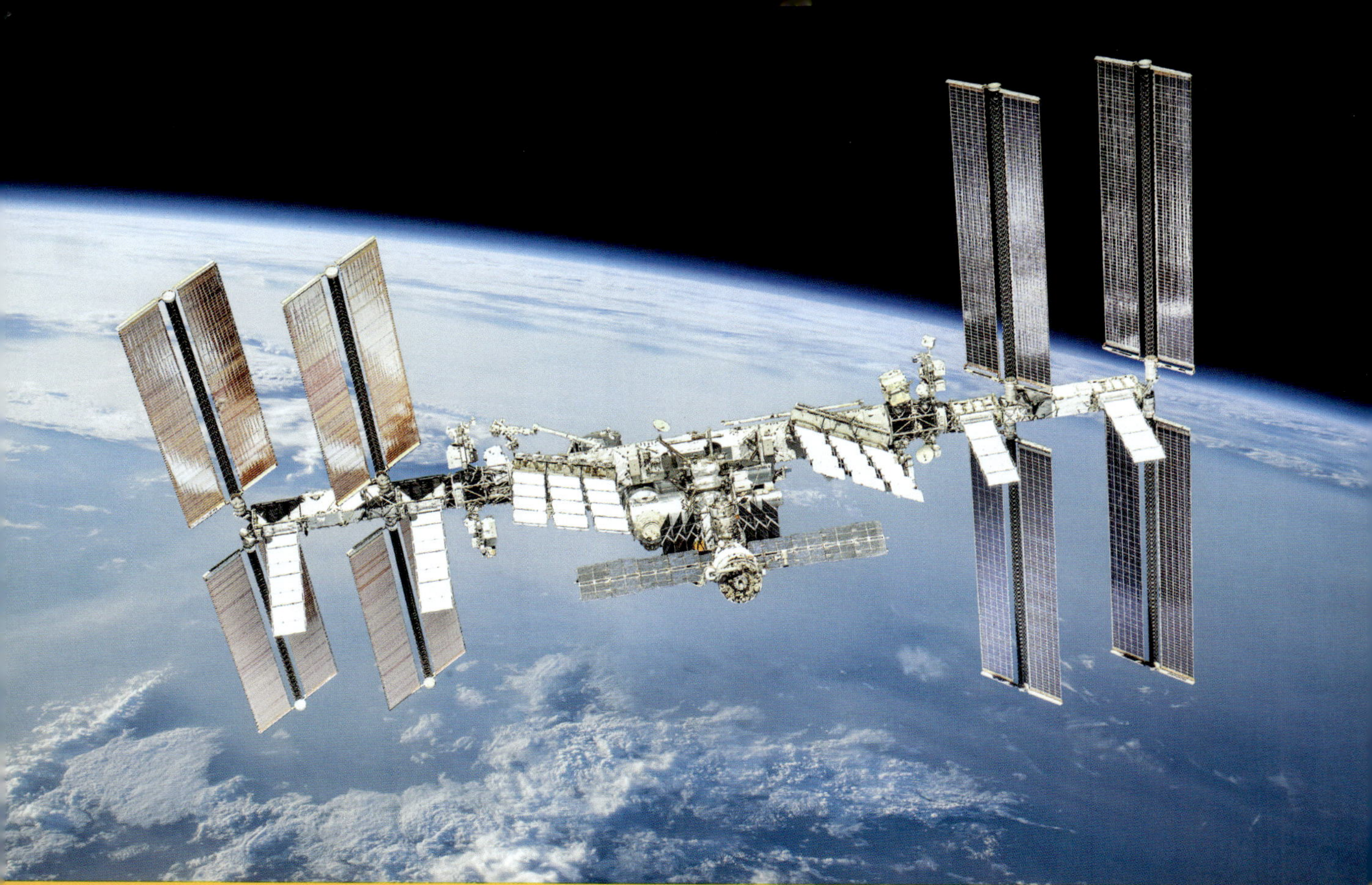

The ships dock here.

This is where astronauts live while in space.

The astronauts float in space. They do all of their work this way!

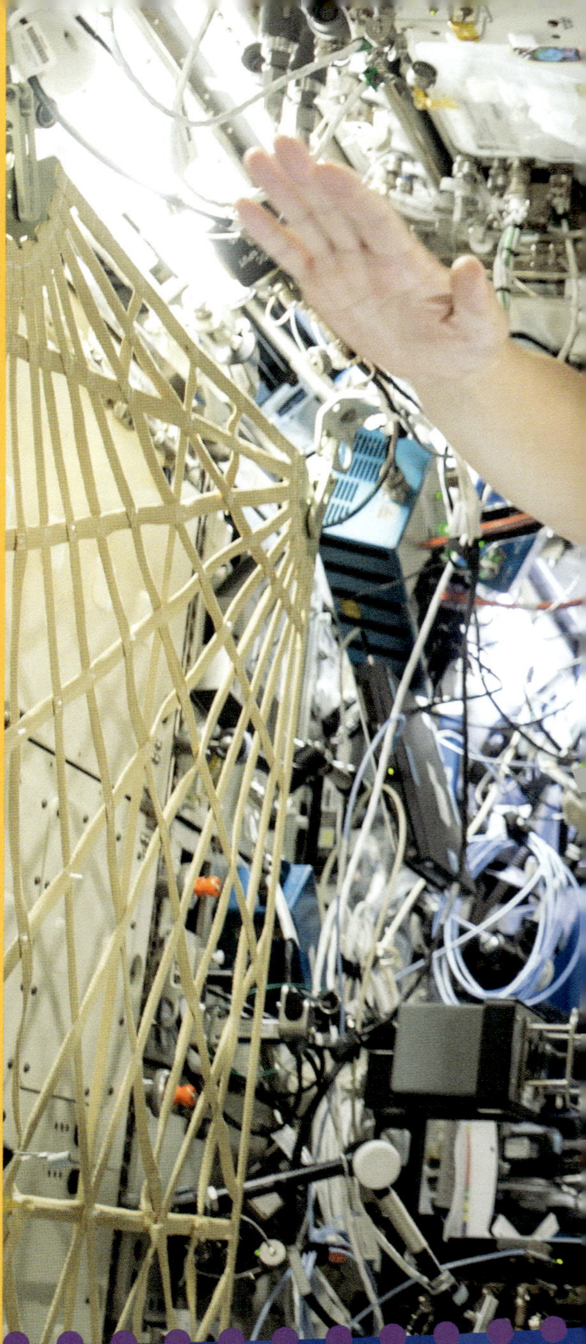

Do you know why astronauts float in space?

Astronauts eat three meals a day in space. The food floats too!

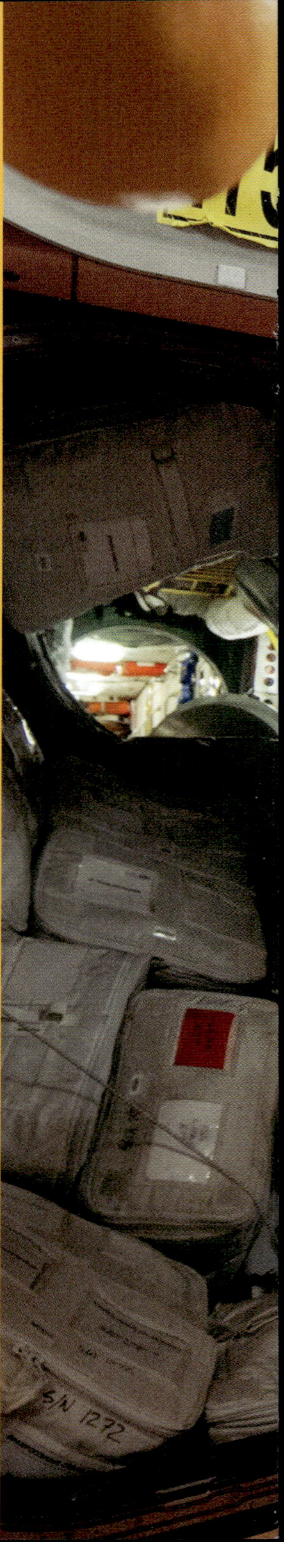

EXIT
28000
km/h
UND

STBD DECK
IMV VALVE

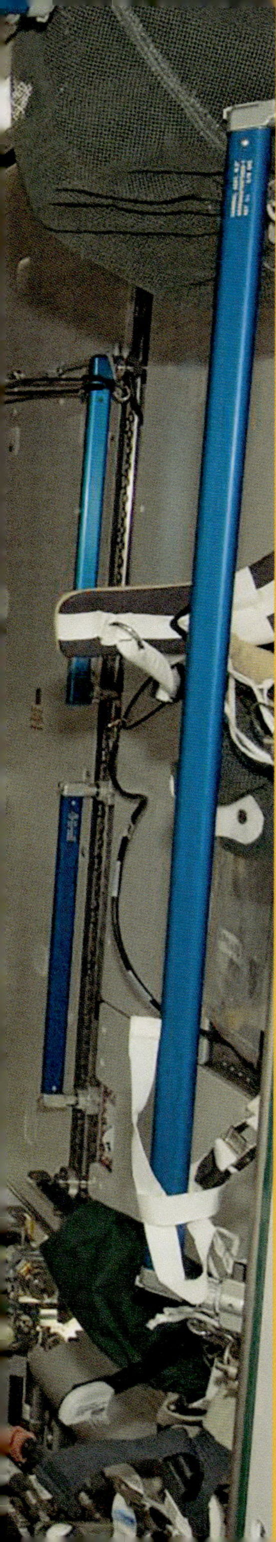

Astronauts also run in space. They must keep their bodies strong.

Sometimes astronauts
go outside.
This is called
a space walk.

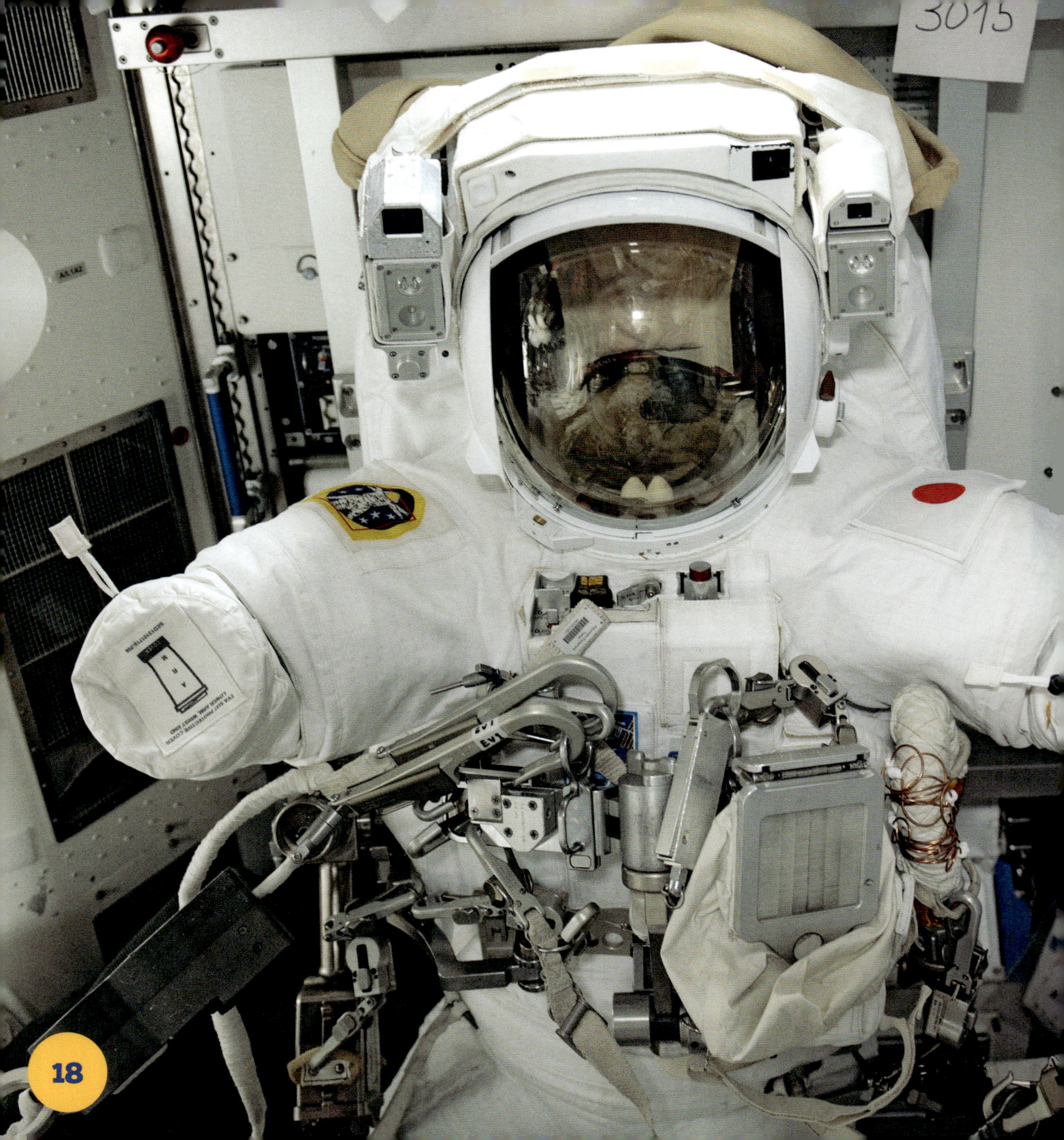

Astronauts wear space suits on space walks. The suits take 45 minutes to put on!

The astronauts return to Earth. They land in the ocean!

You Connect!

What is something you like about astronauts?

Do you think you would like living in space?

What do you think would be hard about being an astronaut?

STEM Snapshot

Encourage students to think and ask questions like scientists. Ask the reader:

What is something you learned about astronauts?

What is something you noticed about life in space?

What is something you still want to learn about astronauts?

Photo Glossary

astronaut

rocket

space suit

space walk

Learn More

Cruz, Aneta. *Astronaut Training*. New York: Boyds Mills Press, 2021.

Lovitt, Chip. *My Little Golden Book about the First Moon Landing*. New York: Golden Books, 2019.

Meltzer, Brad. *I Am Neil Armstrong*. New York: Dial Books for Young Readers, 2018.

Index

Photo Acknowledgments

The images in this book are used with the permission of: © dima_zel/iStockphoto, p. 8; © NASA, pp. 4–5, 9, 12–13, 16–17, 18–19, 23 (astronaut, space suit, space walk); © NASA Ames, pp. 14–15; © NASA/Bill Ingalls, pp. 6–7, 23 (rocket); © NASA Johnson/Flickr, pp. 10–11; © NASA/Josh Valcarcel, p. 20.

Cover Photo: © NASA.

Design Elements: © Mighty Media, Inc.

Lerner Publications Company
An imprint of Lerner Publishing Group, Inc.
241 First Avenue North
Minneapolis, MN 55401 USA

For reading levels and more information, look up this title at www.lernerbooks.com.

Main body text set in Mikado a Medium.
Typeface provided by Hannes von Doehren.

Library of Congress Cataloging-in-Publication Data

Names: Leed, Percy, 1968- author.
Title: Astronauts : a first look / Percy Leed.
Description: Minneapolis, MN : Lerner Publications, [2023] | Series: Read about space (read for a better world) | Includes bibliographical references and index. | Audience: Ages 5–8 | Audience: Grades K–1 | Summary: "Astronauts live and work in space. Easy-to-read text and fascinating photos give readers a first look at these space travelers"— Provided by publisher.
Identifiers: LCCN 2021045351 (print) | LCCN 2021045352 (ebook) | ISBN 9781728459264 (library binding) | ISBN 9781728464312 (paperback) | ISBN 9781728462165 (ebook)
Subjects: LCSH: Astronauts—Juvenile literature. | Life support systems (Space environment)—Juvenile literature.
Classification: LCC TL793 .L3138 2023 (print) | LCC TL793 (ebook) | DDC 629.4—dc23

LC record available at https://lccn.loc.gov/2021045351
LC ebook record available at https://lccn.loc.gov/2021045352

Manufactured in the United States of America
1 - CG - 7/15/22

Read for a Better World™

What do you know about astronauts?

READ ABOUT SPACE

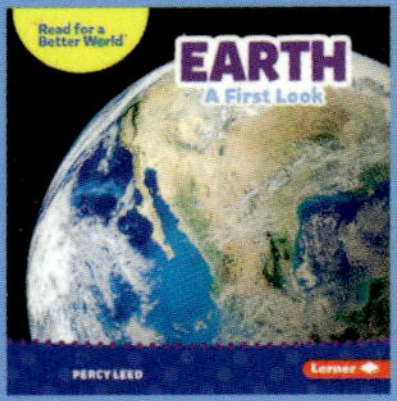

Learn more about Read for a Better World Books at lernerbooks.com/readbetterbooks

ISBN 978-1-7284-6431-2
90000
9 781728 464312

Lerner™
www.lernerbooks.com
GRL: J